A Political Diary

for Jordan,

with best wishes

Bob Keighton

ROBERT KEIGHTON

PAGE PUBLISHING, INC.
Conneaut Lake, PA

First originally published by Page Publishing 2021

ISBN 978-1-64701-601-2 (pbk)
ISBN 978-1-64701-602-9 (digital)

Printed in the United States of America

ACKNOWLEDGMENTS

I wish to thank Page Publishing and Harvy Robbins for their contributions to the preparation of this book.

It was 1944, and President Franklin Roosevelt was running for an unprecedented fourth term. I was thirteen years old and went to hear President Roosevelt deliver a campaign speech at the ballpark in Philadelphia. My memory is that the ballpark was filled to capacity. The president came into the ballpark in an open car, and I do not believe that he was wearing a hat. (Unbeknownst to the public, President Roosevelt was in poor health.)

FDR, as he was known, was introduced to loud applause and began his speech with the words, "My friends, my friends, it is good to be back in Philadelphia."

Roosevelt's opponent in 1944 was Thomas E. Dewey, the governor of New York. (He served from 1943 until 1957.) Some believed that Dewey had a rather cold personality. After shaking hands with Dewey, one person said it was like shaking hands with a frozen chocolate eclair. In November, FDR won the election with 432 electoral votes to Dewey's 99.

As a result of Roosevelt's success, an effort was made by Republicans to limit the president's ability to serve four terms. The Twenty-Second Amendment, enacted in 1957, stated that "no person shall be elected to the office of the president more than twice." The first president subject to the Twenty-Second Amendment was a Republican, Dwight Eisenhower. A very popular figure, he probably could have had a third term except for the fact that he was barred by the Twenty-Second Amendment.

A few years after hearing FDR, I met Mrs. Roosevelt at a reception. She was then in her sixties, and I waited in a long line to meet her. When I shook hands with her, I thought my hand was going to come off.

I said, "Mrs. Roosevelt, you have a very strong handshake." She replied, "I have learned from long experience that if I don't shake first, my hand is gone by the end of the evening." I felt her grip for some time afterward.

When I was in college, I attended a conference of Students for Democratic Action at Bard College in New York. Mrs. Roosevelt was one of the founders of the parent organization, Americans for Democratic Action. While attending the conference, we were invited to meet Mrs. Roosevelt at her home, Val-Kill. Mrs. Roosevelt came out of her home, sat on a rock, and talked with us for nearly an hour.

In 1952, President Truman was campaigning for Adlai Stevenson, the Democratic candidate for president, and gave a speech in Philadelphia. I went to hear him with a fellow college student. Following the speech, we went to Market Street, hoping that Truman's motorcade would be taking that route. According to the memory of my fellow student, the motorcade did come along Market Street with

President Truman riding in an open car. My fellow student claimed that we ran right up to the president's car.

At this point, Truman said, "Stop this motorcade. I want to talk to these boys." Truman asked, "How did you like my speech?" We replied, "It was wonderful." Truman said, "Drive on." (I have only a vague memory of this event and am relying on the memory of my fellow student.)

Many years later, when I was teaching at Curry College in Massachusetts, my colleague, Dick Sinnott, recounted an experience he had had with Truman. In 1952, Dick Sinnott was working for the Associated Press, and because he knew shorthand, he was asked to take down Truman's remarks when he spoke in Boston in support of Adlai Stevenson. Sinnott sat just below Truman and began taking down his remarks.

Suddenly Truman stopped his speech, looked down at Sinnott, and asked, "What are you doing?" Sinnott replied, "I'm taking down your remarks, Mr. President." Then Truman asked, "What are all those squiggles?" Sinnott responded, "Why, Mr. President, I'm taking down your remarks in shorthand." "Are you any good?" asked Truman. Sinnott said he was pretty good. "Then read it back to me," demanded the president. Sinnott began to read his notes, but Truman interrupted, "You are pretty good. If I were going into the White House instead of going out, I'd take you with me."

In the 1952 election, Dwight Eisenhower, the Republican candidate, soundly defeated his Democratic opponent, Adlai Stevenson. In the electoral college, the vote was 442 votes for Eisenhower to 89 for Stevenson.

For many years, Dick Sinnott had a radio program. On one occasion, his guest on the program was Dapper O'Neil. Appointed to the Boston City Council in 1971, O'Neil was elected fourteen times and served until 1999. Extremely conservative, O'Neil believed that school integration was communist-inspired. He never traveled anywhere without a handgun.

When O'Neil appeared on Dick Sinnott's radio show, several people called in to complain about abortions at Boston City Hospital. While the program continued, a storm approached the radio station. O'Neil, according to Dick Sinnott, had the patience of a flea. When still another call came in complaining about abortions at Boston City Hospital, O'Neil answered by saying, "Lady, when I leave this program, I am going straight to Boston City Hospital, and if they don't do something about abortions, may lightning strike me dead." Just then, lightning struck the radio station, kicking O'Neil over onto the floor. Still holding the live microphone, he shouted, "I fucking don't believe this!"

One of my students worked in O'Neil's political campaign and persuaded him to speak to my class. He was very popular because he gave everyone a ticket to a Red Sox Game.

Previous in his career, Dick Sinnott had been press secretary for Mayor John Collins of Boston. Collins was mayor of Boston from 1960 to 1968. In 1955, he contracted polio and was obliged to use crutches. I wanted to have Sinnott recount his many interesting stories to my evening class at Stonehill College, a religious college near Boston where I was teaching part time. There was one problem: Sinnott had, to put it mildly, a very racy vocabulary, and I was not sure he was an appropriate speaker at a religious school. After some trepidation, I decided to have Sinnott speak to my class although I was very nervous as to what the reaction would be from my students and the college. Earlier in the day of my class, I had to be at Stonehill. To my surprise, I encountered Mayor Collins walking along on his crutches.

"Mayor Collins, what are you doing here?" I asked. Mayor Collins replied, "I'm chairman of the board of trustees of Stonehill College." I said, "That's absolutely wonderful." Mayor Collins probably thought I was complimenting him, but I was really thinking that Sinnot's remarks would not get me into trouble.

In the 1950s, I was working on my doctorate at the University of Pennsylvania. After completing the coursework, I had to take an oral exam, where many members of the political science department came to quiz me on my knowledge. Nearly all the questions were on foreign policy, and I had not taken a single course dealing with foreign policy. As the meeting went on, I grew increasingly desperate for intelligent responses. Suddenly the door of the room opened and in came Professor Robert Strausz-Hupé.

Strausz-Hupé seemed unsteady on his feet, and I wondered if he had fortified himself with a few drinks.

Professor Strausz-Hupé promptly took over the meeting and asked, "Why did Napoleon lose the battle of Waterloo?" I was surprised by the question and gave what I thought was a reasonable answer, but the professor responded, "No. He got up late on the morning of the battle and did not survey the scene as was his custom. And why did he get up late on the morning of the battle?" asked the professor. I said I didn't know. Professor Strausz-Hupé responded, "He ate an omelet the night before that didn't agree with him." His next question was, "Why did the omelet not agree with him?" Again, I professed ignorance. "It was made with a bad egg," said the professor and then added, "you know, Mr. Keighton, it was all because of some chicken that Napoleon lost the battle of Waterloo." At this point, he said, "We have no more time for questions. The meeting is adjourned." Everyone followed Professor Strausz-Hupé out of the room. I was very grateful that the session had ended without any other questions. I later thought that possibly Professor Strausz-Hupé was trying to warn me about the unexpected in life.

In 1980, I was living in Randolph, Massachusetts. That year Ronald Reagan was campaigning for the Republican nomination for president. He spoke to the chamber of commerce, and I was able to wrangle a ticket. At one point in his speech, Reagan said, "I am a hard-line anti-communist, just like Robert Strausz-Hupé." I nearly fell out of my chair. After Reagan became president, he appointed Strausz-Hupé to various diplomatic positions, including ambassador to Belgium.

In 1960, John Kennedy and Lyndon Johnson were both vying for the Democratic nomination for president. One of Johnson's supporters argued that Johnson was better qualified to be president because he had lots of gray in his hair, presumably something that the forty-three-year-old Kennedy did not. Then someone offered the view that Kennedy had lots of gray hair as well which, I thought, seemed highly unlikely.

I spent much of the summer of 1960 in Washington, DC, doing research for my doctoral dissertation. One day, during my stay in Washington, I encountered John Kennedy, then a senator from Massachusetts, in a corridor of the Capitol where he was reading a magazine (whether this was before or after his nomination for president, I do not remember, but at this time, I believe, there was no secret service protection until someone was elected president). I did a little tour around Kennedy to see if he had any gray hairs. Suddenly he realized someone was walking around him.

He looked up and asked, "What the hell are you doing?" I explained that I was looking to see if he had any gray hairs. Kennedy's curiosity was aroused, and he inquired, "Do you see any?" I replied that I did not see any. Then Kennedy said, "I don't think I have any either, but if I get elected president, give me six months in the White House, and I promise you, I will have some gray hairs."

During my Washington summer of 1960, I generally stayed at the Carroll Arms Hotel. One day, I met a young lady in the hotel, and I asked her what she did for a living. She said she worked for the Quorum Club. I had never heard of the club and asked her what it did.

Her answer, "We provide call girls for members of Congress." The Carroll Arms Hotel later became a police station, and the Quorum Club presumably moved elsewhere.

After Kennedy received the Democratic nomination for president in 1960, he surprised many by choosing Lyndon Johnson as his running mate. Johnson was considered more conservative than Kennedy, and his place on the ticket was opposed by many liberals. Since Johnson was from Texas, that was seen as a move to help Kennedy carry the South.

Johnson was first elected to the Senate in 1948 and won by only eighty-seven votes. After this, he was sometimes referred to as "Landslide Lyndon." There were accusations that he had been elected by stolen votes although these accusations were never proven.

At that time, charges of fraud in Texas were not unknown. One story that made the rounds was about two people who went to a cemetery to add names to the voting rolls. They came on a tombstone that had two names on it. One person started to copy down the names, but the other one said, "That's very improper. One tombstone, one vote."

There were many apocryphal stories about Lyndon Johnson. When he was the Senate majority leader, he supposedly acquired an official limousine. His Republican counterpart, Senate minority leader Everett Dirksen, also acquired a limousine. Then Johnson had a telephone installed in his limousine. Not to be outdone, Dirksen had a telephone installed in his limousine. One day, both limousines were headed to the Capitol. Seeing Johnson's limousine up ahead, Dirksen called on his telephone.

"Lyndon, this is Everett. Everett McKinley Dirksen. I'm calling from my private telephone in my private limousine." There was a short pause, and then Johnson replied, "Just a moment, Everett. My other telephone is ringing."

When he became president, Johnson, on a visit to Texas, allegedly took the presidential limousine, managed to evade the secret service, and drove at an excessive rate of speed. Stopped by a state trooper, Johnson rolled down the tinted window. When the state trooper looked in and saw it was President Johnson, he exclaimed, "Oh my god!" According to the story, Johnson replied, "You better believe it."

I moved to Texas in 1960 to take a teaching position at Tarleton College (now Tarleton University). Shortly after my arrival, I attended a campaign rally for the Kennedy-Johnson ticket where Lyndon Johnson was the main attraction. The rally was held in a large tent, and I paid a donation to the campaign of $2.50. For my money, I was rewarded with baked beans and stale potato chips. Several speakers addressed the audience, including one man who spoke for all but a few minutes of the time reserved for Johnson's TV appearance. When Johnson finally got to speak, he spent much of the time on Kennedy's courage, including the claim that Kennedy, while serving in World War II, deliberately rammed his PT boat into a Japanese destroyer. After the speech, Johnson charged into the crowd and, at one point, grabbed both of my hands in both of his and spoke to each one in turn, apparently thinking I was two different people.

Kennedy defeated his Republican opponent, Richard Nixon, in the 1960 election. The election result was very close—out of more than 68 million votes, Kennedy won in the popular vote by 112,827. Kennedy took 303 electoral votes to 219 for Nixon. The Kennedy-Johnson ticket carried Texas, and this was a key factor in Kennedy's victory. Most people attributed Kennedy's victory to the TV debates he had with Nixon where Kennedy appeared quite poised and confident. Kennedy himself thought that the TV debates made the difference.

Local campaigns in rural Texas were held in an informal manner. The campaign bus pulled into town with the candidate and a country and western band. The candidate spoke for a few minutes and then went into the crowd to shake hands while the band played "You Are My Sunshine" or some other favorite. Then the candidate returned to the bus, and the campaign moved on to another town.

At the time I was in Texas, most voters in that state were Democrats. Republicans were few and far between, and very often, the Republicans did not even run candidates for office. This was before the Civil Rights Act of 1964 and the Voting Rights Act of 1965 that dramatically changed the political complexion of the South and caused many voters to become Republican.

In one statewide race, there seemed to be an endless number of people funning for the same office. When I inquired as to why there were so many, I was told by someone that all you had to do to get your name on the ballot was to pay a $50 filing fee, and according to the person, it was like buying a postage stamp anywhere else.

At one point, a local census was taken. The census taker wanted to know two things: (1) what is your political affiliation; and (2) what is your religion? The census taker arrived at one professor's house after the professor had spent an afternoon of heavy drinking.

When the census taker asked the professor about his political affiliation, he replied, "I'm a Democrat." The census taker seemed quite pleased. "And what is your religion?" asked the census taker. The professor replied, "I'm a druid." The census taker gave a terrified look and quickly exited the house.

When the census taker arrived at my apartment the following day, he asked about my political affiliation.

When I said, "I'm a Democrat," he gave what I took to be an approving smile.

"And what is your religion?" he asked. I replied, "I'm a Quaker," a religion that was apparently unfamiliar to him. With a horrified look, he pocketed his pencil and made a very hasty exit. I never saw the census taker again.

It was my aim to have people of varied political persuasions speak at the college, but one person was apparently too controversial. This was General Walker who had resigned from the military after attempting to influence the votes of his troops. General Walker lived in Dallas where he flew the American flag upside down, apparently as a protest against government policies. Unable to have the general at the college, I had the idea of bringing some of my students to his home. General Walker readily agreed, but just days before our scheduled visit, someone, on April 10, 1963, took a shot at General Walker when he was sitting in his living room. General Walker canceled our planned visit, saying, "I'm not seeing anyone right now." Several years later, I heard that the shooter may have been Lee Harvey Oswald, the man who later killed President Kennedy.

In 1963, I took a position at Babson Institute (now Babson College) in Massachusetts. The founder, Roger Babson, was still living then well into his eighties (he died in 1967 at the age of ninety-one). Mr. Babson was very wealthy and had his own chauffeur. I often ate at the restaurant where Mr. Babson also dined.

On one occasion, when he entered the restaurant, a lady exclaimed, "Oh, Mr. Babson, I want you to know that my grandfather is ninety-five years old and still drives his own car." To this, Mr. Babson replied, "I certainly feel sorry for the pedestrians on the street."

Mr. Babson had three rules for living: (1) always obey your mother; (2) never borrow money; and (3) never drink alcohol. In 1940, Mr. Babson had been a candidate for president on the Prohibition ticket, a party that had fielded presidential candidates since 1872. In 1940, the Prohibition ticket received 57,925 votes. When teaching at what was then an all-male student body, it was clear to me that the students paid little attention to Mr. Babson's prohibition against alcohol.

The students at Babson were generally conservative. One was a member of the ultraconservative John Birch Society. My student asked if I would be willing to attend a meeting of the John Birch Society in Dartmouth, Massachusetts, a meeting that was open to the public.

I asked him who they were having as a speaker, and he said, "General Walker." I told my student that I would definitely be there. The topic of General Walker's speech was that the Kennedy assassination was a plot by the United Nations. The hall was filled to capacity by supporters and opponents of the John Birch Society. A photographer positioned himself near General Walker and attempted to take his picture. General Walker clearly did not like this idea and kept gesturing for the photographer to go away. After the third attempt, General Walker suddenly punched him. The photographer punched back, and pretty soon, the entire audience was in a melee. I made a hasty exit. The next day, my student said, "Dr. Keighton, you missed all the excitement."

Another of my students was an ardent supporter of Barry Goldwater, a conservative senator from Arizona who was campaigning for the Republican nomination for president in 1964. My student was in the habit of putting Goldwater bumper signs on my car, which I had to frequently remove. Although I was not in accord with the political views of Goldwater, I agreed to go with him to New Hampshire to hear Goldwater address a campaign rally. My recollection was that the rally took place in a large hall in Manchester. When we arrived at the hall, we saw several prominent-looking people sitting at the front of the hall on a platform. My student went up to the dignitaries on the platform and explained that he was an official from someplace in New Hampshire. He was immediately ushered to a seat on the platform. A man who claimed to be a Hollywood movie star was holding the microphone and was leading cheers for Goldwater, who had yet to enter the hall. My student asked if he could lead one cheer for Goldwater, and the man holding the microphone agreed, but once in control of the microphone, my student refused to relinquish it. When Senator Goldwater entered the hall and went up on the platform, he apparently assumed that my student was in charge. After the speech, my student motioned for me to come up on the platform. He introduced me to Goldwater by saying, "Senator Goldwater, I want you to meet Dr. Keighton. He is one of your biggest financial backers in New Hampshire." Senator Goldwater appeared overjoyed. Goldwater went on to capture the 1964 Republican nomination for president. He was defeated in the presidential race by President Lyndon Johnson. The vote in the electoral college was 486 for Johnson to 52 for Goldwater.

The last time I saw Goldwater was some years later when I was teaching at Curry College in Massachusetts. I had taken some of my students to Washington, and while there, we had an evening meeting with Congressman James Shannon at someone's elegant apartment. It was about eleven at night when we left, and to our surprise, Senator Goldwater emerged from the same apartment complex. Goldwater walked in a very unsteady manner toward the street. He did not stop at the curb but continued into the street just as a car came rapidly toward him. With a colleague, we pulled Goldwater out of the way in the nick of time. Said Goldwater, "Thank you. You saved my life!" Fortunately, he did not remember that I was one of his biggest financial backers in New Hampshire.

Sometime in 1963, I went to hear Malcolm X speak in Boston. He was one of the most charismatic speakers I ever heard. At the end of his speech, he entertained questions. It was not evident to me, but one questioner seemed to think he had a reddish tinge to his hair.

He asked, "How can you call yourself a black man when you have red hair?" Malcolm X had a ready reply, "It's not my fault my grandmother was raped by a white plantation owner."

In 1966, I began a teaching position at Curry College, and I moved to Randolph, Massachusetts. Shortly after I moved there, I went to the town hall to register to vote. The person I encountered in the registrar's office told me it was necessary to take a literacy test. In actuality, the literacy test had been outlawed by the Voting Rights Act of 1965, but I was curious to see what the test was, so I did not say anything. "Read the Constitution," said the person. I got as far as "We the people" when she said, "You passed." I told her that the literacy test was illegal, and she gave me a very surprised look.

A few months after moving to Randolph, I met a state senator. The senator made it a point to read the funeral notices for people in his district who had passed away. Whether he had known the person or not, he attended the funeral. When the former Randolph Chief of Police died, I attended the funeral since I knew a member of the family. It was a short walk from my apartment to the church. Naturally, the state senator showed up. After the funeral, a line of cars headed down the main street to the cemetery. I was walking home along the main street when a car window in the funeral procession suddenly came down, and I heard the state senator exclaim, "Hi, Bob. I'm having a wonderful time."

When I was campaigning to be a town meeting member, I went house to house to secure votes. Arriving at one house, a man asked my name. Then he wanted to know how I spelled it. After I obliged, his response was, "Of course, I'll vote for you. Your last name begins with K, and so does mine."

At the time, I began teaching at Curry. The biggest crisis in the nation was the Vietnam War. Nearly every day, there was a protest against the war on the Curry campus. The protests went on regardless of the weather. The unofficial center for student protests in Massachusetts was Brandeis University. One of the Curry students called up students at Brandeis and informed them that Curry students were having a protest against the Vietnam War.

A Brandeis student replied, "Don't be ridiculous. Curry students never protest anything." A delegation of Brandeis students came to Curry to check the matter out. When they arrived, much to their surprise, a very active protest was going on.

When I arrived at Curry in 1966, the voting age was twenty-one. Students made the argument that if they were old enough to fight, they should be able to vote, and this led to a widespread effort to lower the voting age to eighteen. On college campuses, it was a hot-button issue. When I took some of the students to Washington, where we met with the local congressman James Burke, one of my students asked the congressman how he felt about lowering the voting age to eighteen.

Mr. Burke replied, "I am totally opposed to that. Eighteen is much too young." The next year, I again took some of my students to Washington, and we had another meeting with the congressman. A student posed the same question, and the congressman replied, "I think it should be lowered to twenty, but eighteen is much too young." The same conversation occurred the following year, and the congressman thought that the age should be lowered to nineteen. The next year, we met with Mr. Burke again, but none of my students raised the idea of eighteen-year-olds having the right to vote. I decided to ask him the question. "Mr. Burke, what do you think about eighteen-year-olds getting the right to vote?" The congressman replied, "That's a wonderful idea. I'm all in favor of that." The voting age was finally lowered to eighteen with the passage of the Twenty-Sixth Amendment in 1971.

One of my students decided he wanted to move his voting registration from Connecticut to Massachusetts since he lived in Massachusetts for most of the year. The student was very bright and served as head of the student government. He liked to ride a motorcycle but was in an accident that injured his leg and forced him to walk with a decided limp. When he went to the Milton registrar's office at the town hall to change his registration, he was told, "We don't serve drunks in this office."

The student returned to Curry and was quite irate. A contentious debate occurred between the town and the college. Eventually, the town gave in, and the student was allowed to change his registration from Connecticut to Massachusetts. After that, such changes became routine.

In 1968, I went to New Hampshire before the presidential primary day with a student who was quite anxious to meet Richard Nixon, then running for the Republican presidential nomination. We found the candidate at the Republican campaign headquarters. In contrast to his poor appearance in 1960 in the first presidential debate with John Kennedy, Nixon looked quite good.

My student exclaimed in an excited manner, "I've got to shake hands with Nixon." After doing so, he seemed to be in a state of euphoria. "I'm so excited I'm not going to wash my hands for a year." Then he said, "Dr. Keighton, you just have to shake hands with Nixon." Reluctantly, I agreed to do so. After that happened, my student exclaimed, "Wasn't that great?" I replied, "I will be washing my hands every five minutes for a year."

Nixon went on to secure the Republican nomination for president and went on to defeat his Democratic opponent, Hubert Humphrey, in the presidential election. The vote in the electoral college was 301 for Nixon and 191 for Humphrey and 46 for third-party candidate George Wallace.

In 1970, President Nixon had an opportunity to fill a vacancy on the Supreme Court. The first person he chose, Clement Haynsworth, was not confirmed by the Senate. Then Nixon nominated G. Harrold Carswell of Georgia. Carswell was a controversial choice. In 1948, he ran for the

Georgia legislature as a segregationist and white supremacist candidate. In addition, many viewed him as a mediocre talent. Senator Roman Hruska of Nebraska added fuel to the controversy by saying, "Even if he is mediocre, there are a lot of mediocre judges and people and lawyers. They are entitled to a little representation, aren't they…? We can't have all Brandeises, Frankfurters, and Cardozos." The Senate vote on Carswell was expected to be close and Nixon's vice president, Spiro Agnew, arrived in the Capitol in case it was necessary to break a tie vote.

At the time, I was in Washington with some of my students, and we went to the Senate gallery to watch the debate on the Carswell nomination. A long line of people was waiting to get into the Senate gallery, and once in, we were only allowed to stay for ten minutes. It seemed likely that by the time we waited in line again, the vote for Carswell would be long over. We decided to position ourselves at the door of the Capitol where we thought Vice President Agnew was likely to emerge. As it turned out, Agnew's vote was not needed, and the Carswell nomination went down to defeat by a vote of 51 to 45. Agnew emerged from the doorway where we were standing and proceeded to walk to his limousine that was parked a short distance away.

As he was about to enter the limousine, a man shouted, "Better luck next time, Spiro." Agnew turned around, got very red in the face, and shook his fist at the man. Then he disappeared into the limousine, and it drove quickly away.

In 1972, George McGovern became the Democratic candidate for president. He announced that his running mate would be Thomas Eagleton, a senator from Missouri. Shortly after the Democratic convention had adjourned, it was revealed that Eagleton had at one time undergone psychiatric care and had taken electric shock treatment. Faced with the prospect of losing political and financial support, McGovern dropped Eagleton from the ticket, and he was replaced by Sargent Shriver. At the time this happened, I was in Washington where one of my former students, then attending graduate school, had secured a position running the Senate elevator. As I was talking with him, he handed me a very large McGovern-Shriver campaign button. I was amazed that he had one since it was only a very short time after Shriver had been added to the ticket.

"Put it on, Dr. Keighton," said my former student. "I want to see what it looks like on you." No sooner had I put it on when the elevator opened, and out came Senator Thomas Eagleton. Seeing the new campaign button, he gave a devastating look and walked away. I thought that if I ever saw him again, I would get a McGovern-Eagleton button to cheer him up, but I never saw him again.

Nixon went on to win the 1972 election over McGovern. The vote in the electoral college was 520 for Nixon and 17 for McGovern. Nixon carried every state except for Massachusetts. The district of Columbia also voted for McGovern. When Nixon's political stock began to fall because of the Watergate scandal, bumper stickers appeared in my state that said, "Don't blame me. I'm from Massachusetts."

When Tip O'Neill was the majority leader of the US House of Representatives, he received an honorary degree from Curry College. During the commencement, he said to me, "I'm going to be the next Speaker of the House." In a skeptical voice, I said, "You are?" O'Neill replied, "You wait and see." As it turned out, O'Neill became the next Speaker of the House.

Some time after he became Speaker, I took a group of my students to Washington. As we were standing on the steps of the Capitol, we saw a limousine down below. One of my students exclaimed, "Why, it's Speaker O'Neill." The Speaker was sitting in the back of the limousine with a driver up front. My student went running down the steps of the Capitol, raced up to the limousine, opened the back door, and jumped in next to the startled Speaker who had never seen the student before in his life. Then, to make matters worse, my student said, "It's quite all right, Mr. Speaker. I'm a student at Curry College." I looked for a place to hide, but there was none in sight. Fortunately, O'Neill seemed unfazed and said, "Curry College. They gave me an honorary degree last year. I just love everyone from Curry College." He then proceeded to talk to us for about twenty minutes. Finally, O'Neill said, "I really should be going. I'm keeping President Carter waiting at the White House." It was clearly more important to talk to us than it was to meet with the president of the United State. As O'Neill was fond of saying, "All politics is local."

While O'Neill certainly knew politics, he was apparently less knowledgeable when it came to movie stars. When the movie star Sophia Loren came to Washington, he said to her, "I really enjoyed you in *Bridge on the River Kwai*."

Sophia Loren replied, "But, Mr. Speaker, I wasn't in that movie." O'Neill responded, "If you had been, it would have been a much better movie."

On June 17, 1972, burglars broke into the Democratic headquarters in the Watergate complex in Washington, DC. It was later shown to be an effort to assist President Nixon's reelection campaign. Nixon tried to cover up the burglary by falsely claiming it was a CIA operation. The Watergate scandal eventually led to Nixon's resignation on August 9, 1974.

Beginning in May of 1973, hearings were held by the Senate Watergate Committee, headed by Senator Sam Ervin of North Carolina. Senator Ervin had a folksy exterior that disguised a sharp political mind. When he talked, his eyebrows jumped up and down. One of my students wanted to go to Washington for one principal reason—to see Sam Ervin's eyebrows jumping up and down, but the semester ended before his dream could be realized.

Some months before the Watergate break-in, I was having a conversation with Congressman Robert Drinan of Massachusetts. He astonished me by saying, "There are a lot of crooks in Washington, but the biggest one is in the White House."

The Watergate scandal led to a sense of fear on the part of some people in Washington. It was no wonder since Nixon had established an Enemies List to target his opponents. When I talked to one member of Congress, he suggested we talk at the side of the room, saying, "I'm afraid my telephone might be bugged."

Several years after Watergate, I became involved in an effort to save a historic farm. The farm, known as Prowse Farm, was to play an important role in the 1988 presidential race. There were many reasons why people wanted to save Prowse Farm. A major reason was that it is the site of the Doty Tavern where, in 1774, colonists met to protest the British Coercive Acts. These acts had been passed in response to the Boston Tea Party. One of the acts closed the Port of Boston for all shipping and put a stranglehold on the economy of Massachusetts. Meeting at the Doty Tavern and at two subsequent meetings, colonists drafted the Suffolk Resolves that declared that no obedience was due to these acts and added that they were an attempt by a wicked administration to enslave America. Paul Revere took the Suffolk Resolves to the Continental Congress, then meeting in Philadelphia, where they were adopted by all thirteen colonies. John Adams wrote, "This day convinces me that the colonies will stand by Massachusetts or perish with her."

Prowse Farm was also important as the site of the J. Malcolm Forbes horse farm where, in the 1890s, Forbes introduced the concept of selective breeding to enhance the quality of the trotting horse.

An additional reason why people wanted to save Prowse Farm was that it adjoined a public park known as the Blue Hills Reservations. Prowse Farm came to be known as "the window to the Blue Hills."

In 1975, the owner of the farm, Mrs. Prowse, passed away. She did not specify what should happen to the farm, and a long battle ensued between those who wanted to preserve the farm and a company called Codex Corporation that wanted to use it for its corporate headquarters. An organization was formed, known as the Friends of Prowse Farm, in an effort to save the farm. The organization was headed by Harvey Robbins who had boarded his horse on the farm when Mrs. Prowse was alive. A person of unlimited determination, the president of Codex once said of Harvey Robbins, "Even if they dropped agent orange, Harvey would still be coming."

Prowse Farm is located in Canton, Massachusetts, and the land was zoned as agricultural land. Any development would require a change to limited industrial by the Canton Town Meeting. On two occasions, the town meeting rejected rezoning, but on the third occasion, it passed when the moderator cut off debate after hearing only the prodevelopment side.

Nonresidents of Canton were not allowed in the meeting, and some of us sat in a car outside to await the result. It was quite dark. Suddenly a flashlight came into our car. At the end of the flashlight was a Canton police officer who said, "Let me see your licenses." After inspecting our licenses, he said, "You people don't live in Canton. Get out of town. We don't want you here."

Since I was waiting for one of my students to join me, I hid behind a bush near the road. As I was waiting for my student, a group of teenagers came along the sidewalk and stopped in front of the bush. Several minutes later, a car drove up. The teenagers handed some money to the driver of the car, and he handed a package back in return (probably, I thought, a drug deal). The driver left, but the teenagers continued to stand there. Then a place car drove up, and the police officer started to question the students. I was afraid he would see me and think I was a drug dealer. Apparently satisfied, he finally drove away. After a while, the students moved on. Still later, my student finally arrived; I emerged from behind the bush and said, "Let's get out of here before we end up in jail."

In the town meeting, Codex promised to preserve all the farm buildings but then allowed the property to go into disrepair. I went to the farm to take pictures of the state of the buildings and fences. Just as I was about to take my first picture, a man suddenly emerged from Mrs. Prowes's house and pointed a shotgun at me. As he pursued me with his shotgun, I beat a hasty retreat. As Harvey Robbins later put it, "Keighton ran even faster than when he came in next to last at the Prowse Farm fundraising road race." Codex later demolished most of the farm buildings but claimed it had only destroyed a few chicken coops.

Harvey Robbins and I decided to put the issue of having Prowse Farm on the ballot: "Should Prowse Farm be preserved in its entirety?" Although we were only able to get it on the ballot as a nonbinding vote, we did manage to get it approved as a ballot question in five towns, including the town of Canton. When the votes were tallied, we were able to win by a vote of 36,602 to 13,314 and carried all five towns.

Michael Dukakis had been governor of Massachusetts. Known as "The Duke," he had been defeated for reelection in the Democratic primary by conservative Democrat Ed King. King went on to defeat his Republican opponent Francis Hatch in the general election. King had a clever slogan, "Dump the Duke, down the Hatch, and crown the King."

Dukakis, now out of office, wanted to return as governor. When he saw the nonbinding vote on Prowse Farm, he called us to his home in Brookline and said, "Prowse Farm is my favorite piece of land… Believe me, once back in the office, I will save the farm." He repeated this promise many times during his campaign to return as governor.

One of the strongest advocates for saving Prowse Farm was the star of the Celtics basketball team Dave Cowens. He agreed to do commercials for Dukakis that included such appeals as "Vote for Mike Dukakis. He's a straight shooter."

At one point, Dave Cowens asked me for the name of Paul Revere's horse. He explained that if he knew the name of Paul Revere's horse, Celtics coach Bill Fitch would give him a day off from practice. I finally came up with the name "Brown Beauty," which was not Revere's horse but one he borrowed to make the ride made famous in Longfellow's poem "The Midnight Ride of Paul Revere." Presumably, this was the name Bill Fitch wanted. The day after I gave him the name Brown Beauty, Dave Cowens retired from the Celtics and never got to use the day off from practice. I have never been able to find the actual name of Paul Revere's horse.

There were many legal expenses in the effort to save Prowse Farm. Dave Cowens held a Celtics old-timers game and donated the proceeds to the effort to save Prowse Farm. At halftime, Red Auerbach, the man who had built the Celtics into a successful franchise, was shooting foul shots for the cause. Every time he made a shot, it was $100 for Prowse Farm. He seemed to have a magic touch as he made one basket after another.

At a party in the evening, I met Red Auerbach for the first time. By way of introduction, I said, "Red, if you keep on shooting like that, we'll have to put you on the Celtics." He glared at me as if to say, "What do you mean? I am the Celtics."

The Friends of Prowse Farm gave a maximum effort to elect Michael Dukakis. This time, he defeated Ed King in the Democratic primary and went on to defeat the Republican candidate John Sears in the general election.

Once in office, Dukakis lacked any plan to save Prowse Farm. He found objections to every plan that was proposed. Finally, he agreed to pursue a lawsuit to take the Farm by eminent domain, but when the Supreme Judicial Court ruled in 1984 that he could take the Farm, Dukakis refused to act. Instead, he allowed the development of the Farm by Codex Corporation to go forward.

Harvey Robbins heard from a Dukakis aide that the governor planned to run for president and this may have influenced his decision. When confronted by this plan, Dukakis said, "Me, President, you're crazy." In 1987, Dukakis announced that he would be seeking the Democratic nomination for president.

Harvey Robbins and I were determined to keep Dukakis from becoming president. The first stop for the Democratic nomination was the Iowa caucus, and we wrote letters to various newspapers in Iowa. The result of the Iowa Caucus was 31.3 percent for Gephardt, 26.7 percent for Paul Simon, and 22 percent for Dukakis. The rest of the candidates were in single digits.

Then the race moved on to the New Hampshire primary. Harvey and I printed up a flier that we passed out at a debate. The flyer had the heading "Mike Dukakis— what you see is not what you get." We handed one to John

Chancellor who gave the NBC national news and heard him say in his evening commentary a few nights later, "What you see in politics is not always what you get." Despite our efforts, Dukakis led the field in the New Hampshire primary with 37 percent.

As the political campaign went on Harvey Robbins wrote a book about the role Dukakis played with respect to Prowse Farm. Appropriately enough, it was called *Betrayal*. A publisher was secured with the aid of former Massachusetts Governor Ed King. We had opposed Ed King when he was governor but now had come together to keep Dukakis from becoming president.

In the summer of 1988, Dukakis received the Democratic nomination for president. The Republican Convention met in August in New Orleans and nominated George H. W. Bush, who had been Reagan's vice president.

During the summer of 1988, the book *Betrayal* was still in the process of publication. Harvey Robbins and I decided to go to New Orleans, seeing an opportunity to advertise the book, but the publisher was not enthusiastic about the trip: "You can go to New Orleans if you have nothing better to do."

The publisher had many conservative connections. He secured an invitation for Harvey and myself to attend a reception for the new editor of the conservative publication National Review. While there, I encountered Vernon Walters who was ambassador to the United Nations (he served from 1985 to 1989). To open the conversation, I said that I heard he was fluent in thirty languages, but he said it was only seven. I did not extend the conversation as he had a habit when talking of spraying all over my face. At one point, a hostess came up to him and asked if he wanted "some of our famous New Orleans Shrimp." Replied Walters, "I hate shrimp." So much for diplomacy.

The publisher of *Betrayal* wanted us to give a prepublication copy to Richard Viguerie, a conservative political figure who was living in a hotel. As we waited in the lobby for Mr. Viguerie, a number of young ladies were walking around. Observed Harvey, "They're all so attractive." We both paused and looked at one another, wondering what kind of house this possibly was.

Then a seductively attired woman came down the stairs and said, "I am Mr. Viguerie's secretary, and I am here to take the book to him." Then, the book in hand, she disappeared up the stairs.

At our motel, we received a phone call at seven o'clock each morning from former Massachusetts' governor Ed King. He wanted to know the status of the book *Betrayal*. We called it our wake-up call from the governor. In view of the fact that we had strongly opposed him as governor, this was an interesting change and supports the view that politics make strange bedfellows.

We had no credentials to get on the convention floor, but we brazenly walked past three checkpoints, literature in hand, and greeted each of the security people guarding the entrance. Once in, we distributed our literature.

On August 17, George H. W. Bush received the Republican nomination for president. Shortly after, we returned to Massachusetts, the book *Betrayal* was finally published.

During the election campaign, I received a call from Warren Brookes whose column appeared in some sixty newspapers around the country, including the *Boston Herald*. He asked me about the issue of Prowse Farm. Somehow he learned that I was a Democrat who planned to vote for George Bush and asked, "Can I mention that in my column?"

I readily agreed. When the column appeared in the Boston Herald, many members of the Democratic Town Committee in Randolph were upset with me, and there was talk of kicking me from the committee. Said one member, "If he plans to do that [vote for Bush], he should face the music." Any plans to kick me out were abandoned when the press showed up at the meeting, and the committee apparently feared that Dukakis would get negative publicity.

The issue of party loyalty was reminiscent of a story attributed to John Kennedy who was elected president in 1960. Asked if he had voted the straight Democratic ticket, Kennedy supposedly said, "Sometimes party loyalty expects too much."

Today party attachment is not as strong as it once was, but in the past, it was very common. In 1936, the popular Democrat Franklin Roosevelt was campaigning for a second term. Someone in New York City was running for a minor office on the Democratic ticket at the same time. He hired a man named Shorenstein to run his campaign, but Shorenstein did absolutely nothing. In desperation, he went to Shorenstein's office and demanded to know why he was not doing anything.

Shorenstein replied, "Have you ever watched the ferry boat come into Staten Island? When it comes to Staten Island, it brings all the garbage and refuses in with it. Stop worrying. Franklin D. Roosevelt is your ferry boat." Sure enough, election day came, and the man went into the office on the coattails of Franklin Roosevelt.

During the 1988 presidential election, a prominent Massachusetts politician said, "We should all vote for Dukakis because we live in Massachusetts." Under this theory, if the candidate was a prominent drug dealer, we should still vote for the person.

Election night, November 8, came, and Bush emerged as the winner. The electoral vote was 426 for Bush and 111 for Dukakis. Bush received 53.4 percent of the popular vote to 45.6 percent for Dukakis. The day after the election, Dukakis met with his supporters for the final time at a hotel in Boston. Harvey Robbins decided to go there and stand at the end of the curved hotel driveway while Dukakis waved goodbye to his supporters and then entered a limousine to take him to his home in Brookline. The limousine moved slowly along the curved driveway. When it reached the end of the driveway, Dukakis automatically waved to the figure who was standing there, unaware it was Harvey Robbins, but Harvey ran up to the window of the limousine and held the book *Betrayal* next to it. Dukakis dropped his hand, and the limousine went on its way.

The last time I saw George H. W. Bush was in 1997 when he came to the dedication of his birthplace in Milton, Massachusetts. Bush had been in the habit of taking a parachute drop every year on his birthday. On this occasion, he joked that he planned to come in by parachute but said if that happened, his wife, Barbara, declared that there would be an immediate divorce.

When Dukakis made his decision to allow construction at Prowse Farm, he presented it as a compromise when, in fact, it had already been stipulated that the open portion of the land would not be developed. The friends of Prowse Farm have established a museum in the house that belonged to Mrs. Prowse and have sponsored events at the farm that have raised more than $37 million for charity.

ABOUT THE AUTHOR

Dr. Robert Keighton is a professor of politics and history at Curry College in Milton, Massachusetts. He received his doctorate from the University of Pennsylvania. In collaboration with Harvey Robbins, he is the author of *If You Elect Me President*, an account of the effort to save a historic farm and the subsequent role of the authors in a presidential election.